WEAPONS OF THE 21ST CENTURY

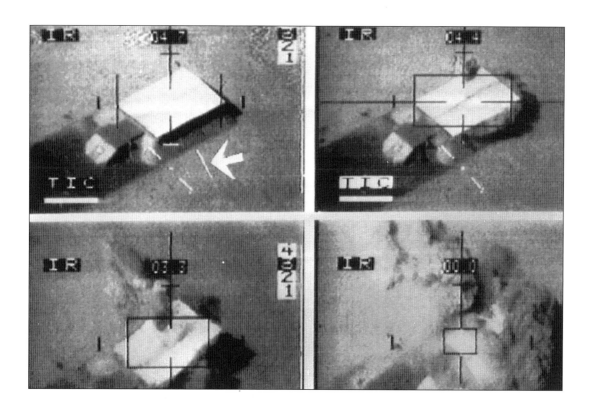

By John Hamilton

VISIT US AT
WWW.ABDOPUB.COM

Published by ABDO & Daughters, an imprint of ABDO Publishing
Company, 4940 Viking Drive, Suite 622, Edina, Minnesota 55435.
Copyright ©2004 by Abdo Consulting Group, Inc. International
copyrights reserved in all countries. No part of this book may be
reproduced in any form without written permission from the publisher.

Printed in the United States.

Edited by: Tamara L. Britton and Kate A. Conley
Graphic Design: Arturo Leyva, David Bullen
Cover Design: Castaneda Dunham, Inc.
Photos: Corbis, Defense Image Digest, Department of Defense,
Digital Stock

Library of Congress Cataloging-in-Publication Data

Hamilton, John, 1959-
        Weapons of the twenty-first century / John Hamilton.
          p. cm. -- (War in Iraq)
        Includes index.
        Summary: Describes United States military equipment and weapons of the twenty-first century.
        ISBN 1-59197-501-8
          1. United States--Armed Forces--Weapons systems--Juvenile literature. 2. Military
weapons--United States--History--21st century--Juvenile literature. 3. Iraq War,
2003--Equipment and supplies--Juvenile literature. [1. Unites States--Armed
Forces--Weapons systems. 2. Military weapons--United States.] I. Title. II. Series.

UF503.H357 2003
623'.0973'0905--dc21
                                                                    2003050306

TABLE OF CONTENTS

An aviation ordnanceman tightens down the guidance fins on an AIM-9 Sidewinder air-to-air missile loaded onto an F/A-18C Hornet.

THE U.S. ARSENAL

The United States has the most powerful military on the planet, with a clear edge in weapons and information technology. Equally important, more than 200 years of tradition have brought superiority in military leadership and soldier skills. These two factors—highly trained human talent and high technology—create an unchallenged fighting force when unleashed by U.S. military leaders.

U.S. soldiers in the twenty-first century are armed with the most deadly and sophisticated weapons ever seen in combat. These include a fierce array of laser- and Global Positioning System (GPS)-guided bombs, stealth aircraft, Tomahawk cruise missiles, and surveillance drones that track enemy positions in real time.

During the 2003 war in Iraq, casualty rates between coalition and Iraqi forces illustrated the advantage U.S. military power has on the open battlefield. After the first two weeks of the war, U.S. forces suffered 52 dead and 150 wounded. Accident, illness, and friendly fire incidents caused approximately one-third of the deaths. At the same time, Iraqi forces are estimated to have lost thousands of soldiers.

During World War II, approximately one out of every 15 soldiers was killed or wounded. During the first two weeks of the war in Iraq, one out of every 1,485 soldiers was killed or wounded. Though soldiers still risk their lives in combat, improved technology makes today's weapons much more accurate, saving many lives.

A U.S. Air Force F-15 fighter jet flies over the Pacific Ocean.

AIR POWER

The F-15 Eagle is a U.S. Air Force tactical fighter jet. It is maneuverable, can fly in bad weather, and can attack targets both in the air and on the ground. The military calls this kind of aircraft a dual-role fighter.

The F-15 is fitted with sophisticated electronics that allow it to fly low to the ground, day or night, to confuse enemy radar. Its ability to make sharp turns at high speed allows it to evade enemy planes or antiaircraft missiles. Some F-15s have a two-person crew. A pilot flies the plane while a weapons officer sits in back watching computer screens. The weapons officer can track and fire on the enemy, sometimes on several targets at once.

F-15 EAGLE

Primary function: Tactical fighter
Speed: 1,875 mph (3,018 km/h)
Length: 64 feet (20 m)
Wingspan: 43 feet (13 m)
Armament: One 20mm multibarrel cannon, various air-to-air and air-to-ground missiles
Crew: One to two
Cost: $28 to $30 million

F-16 FALCON

Primary function: Multirole fighter jet
Speed: 1,500 mph (2,414 km/h)
Length: 49 feet (15 m)
Wingspan: 33 feet (10 m)
Armament: One 20mm multibarrel cannon, air-to-air combat and air-to-surface attack munitions
Crew: One to two
Cost: $15 to $19 million

The F-16 Fighting Falcon is a multirole Air Force fighter that can attack both air and land targets. It is lightweight and can outmaneuver almost any aircraft produced today. Although the F-16 was designed primarily to attack during the day, modern electronics now allow it to strike at night, even in bad weather.

Air Force pilots consider the F-16 to be the world's best fighter aircraft, along with its closest rival, the Soviet MiG-29. The F-16 can fight its way to a target, drop its bombs, then fight its way back to base. Its arsenal of air-to-ground and air-to-air munitions makes the F-16 one of the most fearsome weapons in the skies.

An F-16 fighter from the Sixty-seventh Fighter Squadron prepares for aerial refueling while on a routine mission.

F/A-18E AND F SUPER HORNET

Primary function: Multirole attack and fighter aircraft
Speed: 1,320 mph (2,124 km/h)
Length: 60 feet (18 m)
Wingspan: 45 feet (14 m)
Armament: One 20mm Vulcan cannon, air-to-air combat and air-to-surface attack munitions
Crew: One to two
Cost: $57 million

The Super Hornet is the newest version of the U.S. Navy and Marine Corps's F/A-18 model. It has been updated with cutting-edge electronic systems, allowing it to carry more smart bombs to attack select targets such as missile sites and command bunkers. These fighters have a greater range and endurance, and they can provide close air support, helping troops on the ground. Hornet jet fighters can take off from land bases or aircraft carriers. They are dual-role strike fighters, designed to attack targets in the air and on the ground in all weather conditions.

During the 2003 war in Iraq, F/A-18 E and F Super Hornets were deployed on the aircraft carrier USS *Abraham Lincoln*. The older F/A-18 Hornets were based on other carriers in the Persian Gulf region.

An F-18 Hornet takes off from the deck of an aircraft carrier.

F-14 TOMCAT

Primary function: Carrier-based multirole strike fighter
Speed: 1,544 mph (2,485 km/h)
Length: 62 feet (19 m)
Wingspan: 64 feet (19.5 m)
Armament: One M61A1/A2 Vulcan 20mm cannon, air-to-air combat and air-to-surface attack munitions
Crew: Pilot and radar intercept officer
Cost: $38 million

The U.S. Navy's F-14 Tomcat is launched from an aircraft carrier. It is a fast and nimble strike fighter. Its main mission is to protect ships from enemy planes, but it is also good at launching precision-guided smart bombs and missiles at enemy targets on the ground. The supersonic, twin-engine jet is outfitted with advanced electronics that can track multiple targets at once.

For flying at slower speeds, the F-14's wings sweep forward, giving the jet added lift. When the F-14's wings sweep back, it can travel at twice the speed of sound.

An F-14 Tomcat from the USS *Harry S. Truman* flies a combat mission in direct support of Operation Iraqi Freedom.

F-117A NIGHTHAWK

Primary function: Attack fighter

Speed: 645 mph (1,038 km/h)

Length: 64 feet (19.5 m)

Wingspan: 43 feet (13 m)

Crew: Pilot only

Cost: $45 million

The Nighthawk is the Air Force's first plane to use stealth technology. Because of its shape and special black paint, the F-117A is nearly invisible to enemy radar. For this reason, it is often used to fly into highly defended enemy territory to bomb radar installations and air defenses, making it safer for other U.S. jets to complete their missions.

The Nighthawk is poorly armed against enemy planes. It depends on its stealthy radar profile, and flying low to the ground for its defense. By the time the enemy realizes it is under attack, the Nighthawk has usually already dropped its payload and left the scene.

The twin-engine F-117A is about the size of an F-15 Eagle. It carries complex navigational and attack electronics. Nighthawks can carry several types of munitions, but usually deliver two Paveway 2,000-pound (907 kg) laser-guided bombs. They also commonly carry AGM-65 Maverick air-to-surface missiles, or AGM-88 antiradar missiles.

An F-117 Nighthawk stealth fighter deploys a parachute as it lands at Holloman Air Force Base in New Mexico.

AC-130U GUNSHIP

Primary function: Close air support and force protection
Speed: 300 mph (483 km/h)
Length: 98 feet (30 m)
Wingspan: 133 feet (41 m)
Armament: 40mm cannon and 105mm cannon; 25mm gun
Crew: Five officers: pilot, copilot, navigator, fire control officer, electronic warfare officer; and eight enlisted soldiers: flight engineer, television operator, infrared detection set operator, loadmaster, four aerial gunners
Cost: $190 million

The AC-130U is the latest version of the U.S. Air Force's AC-130H, or Spectre, gunship. Its main mission is to protect soldiers on the ground, which is called close air support. The heavily armed AC-130U, or Spooky, is especially valuable at night assisting special operations troops, such as Army Rangers or Delta Force commandos. It also carries out force protection missions, such as escorting convoys and defending air bases.

The Spooky slowly circles the battlefield and tilts downward so gunners can fire out of the side of the aircraft. It carries several types of weapons, including a 25mm Gatling cannon, a 40mm Bofors cannon, and a 105mm howitzer. With an array of sophisticated optics and sensors, it can track and destroy anything on the ground from enemy troops to tanks. It can track and destroy separate targets that are up to one mile (1.6 km) apart.

The AC-130 gunship's primary missions are close air support, air interdiction, and force protection.

A-10 THUNDERBOLT

Primary function: Close air support

Speed: 420 mph (676 km/h)

Length: 53 feet (16 m)

Wingspan: 58 feet (18 m)

Armament: 30mm Gatling gun, up to 16,000 pounds (7,257 kg) of mixed missiles and bombs

Crew: Pilot only

Cost: $9.8 million

The A-10 Thunderbolt is a U.S. Air Force jet specially designed to assist ground troops by destroying enemy tanks and other armored vehicles. This close air-support ability makes it valuable on the battlefield, especially far into enemy territory where other reinforcements aren't available.

The A-10, nicknamed the Warthog by some aviators, flies low to the ground at relatively slow speeds. It can survive direct hits from the enemy, even by armor-piercing and high-explosive ammunition. It is very maneuverable, with highly accurate weapons systems. It can loiter around the battlefield, flying low and slow, picking off the enemy with deadly accuracy.

The A-10 carries a variety of air-to-ground and air-to-air missiles and bombs under its wings. It also is armed with a nose-mounted 30mm Gatling gun, which can fire at 3,000 rounds per minute and can penetrate enemy tanks.

During the Persian Gulf War, the A-10s launched more than 4,500 AGM-65 Maverick missiles.

B1-B LANCER

Primary function: Long-range, multirole, heavy bomber
Speed: 900+ mph (1,448+ km/h)
Length: 146 feet (45 m)
Wingspan: 137 feet (42 m)
Range: 6,400 miles (10,300 km)
Armament: Short-range attack missiles, bombs, and cruise missiles
Crew: Four: aircraft commander, copilot, offensive systems officer, and defensive systems officer
Cost: $283 million

The U.S. Air Force B-1B Lancer is the only U.S. bomber that can fly faster than the speed of sound. It was developed during the Cold War to drop nuclear bombs on the former Soviet Union. Today, the Lancer supplements the U.S. bomber fleet by carrying up to 84 conventional 500-pound (227-kg) bombs, 30 cluster bombs, or 24 precision-guided smart bombs weighing 2,000 pounds (907 kg) each.

The B-1B Lancer flies fast at low altitude, helping it evade enemy radar. It can even operate at night and in bad weather, because of its sophisticated guidance systems that compare the plane's global position with built-in maps of enemy terrain.

The Lancer has a flight range of about 6,400 miles (10,300 km). For missions in the Middle East, it is often launched from the U.S. Naval Support Facility at Diego Garcia, an island in the middle of the Indian Ocean.

A B-1B Lancer soars over Wyoming. The B-1B is a long-range strategic bomber, capable of flying intercontinental missions without refueling.

B-52 STRATOFORTRESS

Primary function: Heavy bomber
Speed: 650 mph (1,046 km/h)
Range: 8,800 miles (14,162 km)
Length: 159 feet (48 m)
Wingspan: 185 feet (56 m)
Armament: 70,000 pounds (31,751 kg) of bombs, mines, and missiles
Crew: Five: aircraft commander, pilot, radar navigator, navigator, and electronic warfare officer
Cost: $53 million

The U.S. Air Force B-52 Stratofortress is a long-range, heavy bomber that can perform several kinds of missions. It started flying in the 1950s, and it saw heavy use dropping bombs during the Vietnam War. Though it is an older plane design, each B-52 has been completely refitted with modern engines, plus electronic guidance and defensive electronics. It plays an important part of any sustained U.S. bombing campaign.

The B-52 has the ability to carry both regular and nuclear bombs. It also carries air-launched cruise missiles. It can carry a heavy load of munitions, and is sometimes used to carpet bomb the enemy with waves of conventional, dumb bombs. During the 2003 war in Iraq, B-52s were launched from bases in England and from Diego Garcia.

The B-52 is a long-range, heavy bomber that can perform a variety of missions. The aircraft's flexibility was evident in Operation Desert Storm.

B-2 SPIRIT

Primary function: Multirole heavy bomber
Length: 69 feet (21 m)
Wingspan: 172 feet (52 m)
Speed: High subsonic
Range: 6,900 miles (11,104 km)
Armament: Conventional or nuclear weapons
Crew: Two pilots
Cost: $1.157 billion

The B-2 Spirit stealth bomber has a wingspan about half the length of a football field. To enemy radar, however, the B-2 looks smaller than a bird. The B-2 has become a much relied upon heavy bomber for the U.S. Air Force. Using stealth technology, it flies heavy bombing missions deep into enemy territory, with no help from friendly fighter jets.

The B-2 has curved surfaces, with no sharp angles that might show up on enemy radar. Every edge and screw is covered with special tape and black paint, which scatters radar signals. Most planes are made with aluminum, but the Spirit bomber is constructed of lightweight graphite. Noisy signals from electronic equipment, which might give the plane's position away, are trapped and absorbed inside the B-2.

Engines are stored deep inside the B-2, and hot exhaust gasses are cooled before they exit through special vents on top of the wings. This makes the B-2 harder to find, even if the enemy is using heat-seeking missiles. The B-2 can also fly up to 50,000 feet (15,240 m), which puts it out of the range of most ground-to-air missiles.

Because they are so stealthy, B-2s are often used as a first-wave attack bomber. They knock out the enemy's command centers and antiaircraft weapons and clear the way for other U.S. forces to enter the battlefield. B-2s can carry several types of bombs, both nuclear and conventional.

B-2 Spirit bombers are easily damaged by hail, freezing rain, and moisture. The fleet of 21 bombers is housed in special hangers at Whiteman Air Force Base in Missouri. A B-2 has a range of about 6,900 miles (11,104 km), which means it can travel around the world with one mid-flight refueling. This range allows the B-2 to strike targets at any point on the globe.

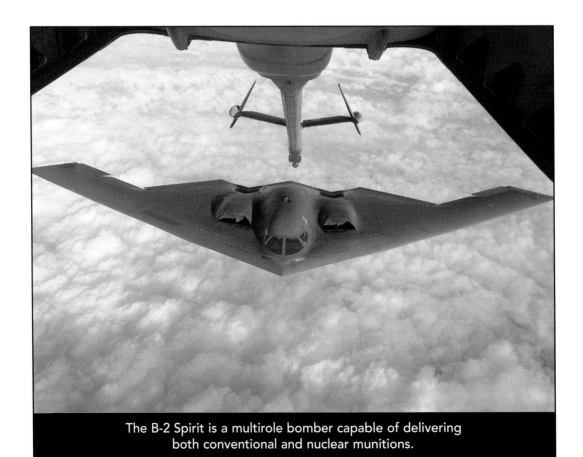

The B-2 Spirit is a multirole bomber capable of delivering both conventional and nuclear munitions.

E-8C JOINT STARS

Primary function: Airborne battle management
Cruising speed: 523 mph (842 km/h)
Crew: Four flight crew, plus mission crew of 15 Air Force specialists and three Army specialists (crew size varies according to mission)
Cost: $244 million

The E-8C Joint Surveillance Target Attack Radar System (Joint STARS or JSTARS) is an advanced airborne targeting and battle management system. E-8C aircraft are Boeing 707-300 jetliners modified with radar and advanced communications systems. The most obvious modification is a 40-foot (12-m) long dome under the forward fuselage. It houses a special radar system called a side-looking phased array antenna.

The radar and computer systems on the E-8C gather and display detailed information about enemy ground forces. A Moving- or Fixed-Target Indicator (MTI) passes on this information in near real time to commanders on the ground. This allows them to quickly and accurately disrupt and destroy enemy forces.

The Joint STARS uses a multimode, side-locking radar to detect, track, and classify moving ground vehicles in all conditions deep behind enemy lines.

NETWORKING PREDATOR DRONES

Primary function: Airborne surveillance, reconnaissance, and target acquisition
Speed: Up to 135 mph (217 km/h)
Range: 454 miles (731 km)
Length: 27 feet (8 m)
Wingspan: 49 feet (15 m)
System Cost: $40 million

The Predator is not just an aircraft. Rather, it is a system of four unmanned drones controlled by pilots and sensor operators. Predators fly slowly over enemy territory, sending back real-time images of terrain, people, buildings, and vehicles. They can stay in the air for 40 hours, gathering information about the enemy without endangering the life of a pilot. The Predator system is connected by a network of line-of-sight radio links or satellite data links for longer ranges.

Fifty-five Air Force personnel operate a linked system of Predators. The drones have a basic crew of one pilot and two sensor operators. Sensors include video and infrared cameras. Each drone can be armed with up to two Hellfire missiles under its wings. Hellfires are accurate, laser-guided missiles capable of destroying armored targets such as tanks.

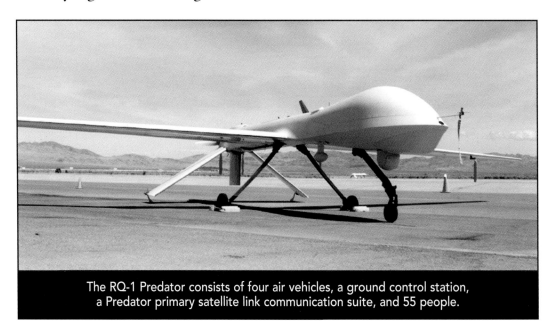

The RQ-1 Predator consists of four air vehicles, a ground control station, a Predator primary satellite link communication suite, and 55 people.

SATELLITES

The United States has an array of military satellites that guide several types of missiles and bombs to their targets. Satellites also provide a treasure trove of useful information on geographical features, military installations, and troop positions.

Most military satellites operate in low, near-polar orbits, traveling between 311 and 1,864 miles (500 and 3,000 km) over Earth. Each satellite orbits the globe about 14 times per day. Satellites scan swaths of ground as they pass overhead using photo-optic, electro-optic, infrared, or radar technology.

The exact number and capabilities of U.S. military satellites is classified top secret, but some educated guesses can be made. The most advanced satellite launched in the past 10 years, the Key Hole series, is said to be able to see objects less than four inches (10 cm) across. The United States has spent about $1.5 billion on Key Hole satellites over the past several years.

Besides providing reconnaissance, today's satellites also serve as a navigational aid. Using a special tracking device, military units can find their exact location on the ground by using GPS satellites. Precision-guided bombs and missiles can also use GPS satellites to find their targets with pinpoint accuracy.

The USS *Harry S. Truman* deploys in support of Operation Iraqi Freedom.

SEA POWER

AIRCRAFT CARRIERS

Since World War II, U.S. naval strategy has revolved around the aircraft carrier. Smaller surface vessels play a supporting role. Aircraft carriers let the United States project power quickly any place in the world. Cruise missiles have changed the way fleets are deployed, but the aircraft carrier is still a critically important part of U.S. military strategy.

Aircraft carriers are too big and important to sail alone. They are part of a larger battle group, which includes many support ships. Guided-missile destroyers and cruisers protect the aircraft carriers, and they can launch offensive attacks with cruise missiles. Fighter planes, especially F-14 Tomcats, are constantly in the air, ready to intercept enemy aircraft that might attack the battle group.

F-14 Tomcats and F/A-18 Hornets are the two most frequently used carrier-based strike fighters sent to attack targets on shore. Aircraft carriers also frequently carry EA-6B Prowler attack aircraft, E-2C Hawkeye command aircraft, S-3A/B Viking marine patrol aircraft, and SH-60 Seahawk antisubmarine helicopters.

Nimitz-class aircraft carriers, such as the USS *Theodore Roosevelt* and the USS *Carl Vinson*, are the largest warships ever built. Each can hold about 6,000 people and 85 aircraft. They are 1,092 feet (333 m) long, which is longer than three football fields. Fully loaded, they can carry up to 97,000 tons (98,556 metric tons). They are powered by nuclear reactors. Each Nimitz-class aircraft carrier costs about $4.5 billion.

ATTACK SUBMARINES

The U.S. Navy's fleet of nuclear-powered attack submarines is designed mainly to seek out and destroy enemy submarines and surface ships. In addition, attack subs collect intelligence and deliver special forces troops to hostile shores.

The U.S. Navy's fleet includes several versions, including Virginia-, Seawolf-, and Los Angeles-class attack subs. Los Angeles-class attack subs, the most numerous type in the navy's fleet, are 360 feet (110 m) long. They have a crew of 133 and cost about $503 million each.

Attack submarines carry many different weapons. In addition to torpedoes and antiship missiles, attack subs also carry Tomahawk cruise missiles.

The USS *Florida* sails off the coast of the Bahamas during
a mission to test its guided-missile capabilities.

GROUND AND AIR CAVALRY WEAPONS

M1A1 ABRAMS TANK

Length: 32 feet (9.75 m)

Weight: 126,000 pounds (57,153 kg)

Crew: Four: commander, gunner, loader, driver

Cost: $4.3 million

The U.S. Army and Marine Corps rely on the M1A1 Abrams as their main battle tank. Many military analysts consider the Abrams to be the best tank ever built. It has a 120mm smoothbore main gun that can destroy most enemy tanks even at long range. The weapons control system uses thermal imaging, night vision, laser rangefinders, and computerized targeting. It works even in haze, fog, and swirling sand.

Despite its large size, the Abrams is fast and mobile. Its armor plating is impenetrable to most antitank weapons, although it does have a vulnerable spot in the rear. During the 2003 war in Iraq, a handful of these tanks were disabled by enemy forces. This was the first time in history that an Abrams tank had been lost in combat.

M1A1 crew members prepare for deployment to southern Iraq
in support of Operation Iraqi Freedom.

M2/3 BRADLEY FIGHTING VEHICLE

Length: 21 feet (6 m)

Weight: 66,000 pounds (29,937 kg)

Crew: Nine: commander, gunner, driver, and six troops

Cost: $3.16 million

The M2/3 Bradley Fighting Vehicle normally carries up to six soldiers into battle. It also supports main battle tanks. The Bradley can speed across the battlefield at up to 42 miles per hour (68 km/h), and is quite agile. Steel armor protects the soldiers inside, while the Bradley can attack with a 25mm M242 chain gun, twin antitank missile launchers, and Stinger surface-to-air missiles.

The army acquired the Bradley Fighting Vehicle in 1981.

WEAPONS OF THE 21ST CENTURY

M109A6 PALADIN

Length: 32 feet (9.75 m)

Weight: 55,000 pounds (24,948 kg)

Crew: Four: commander, gunner, ammunition servers, and driver

Cost: $1.8 million

At first glance, the M109 Paladin howitzer looks like a tank. It is actually a self-propelled artillery weapon that can attack the enemy. It protects its crew from explosives, chemicals, smoke, and nuclear weapons. It can fire its 155mm cannon at targets up to 19 miles (31 km) away.

The M109 has been in the Marine Corps inventory since the mid-1970s.

AH-64D APACHE LONGBOW

Primary function: Multimission attack helicopter

Speed: 189 mph (304 km/h)

Armament: 30mm cannon and Hellfire antitank missiles or 70mm rockets

Crew: Two

Cost: $17 million

The U.S. Army uses the AH-64D Apache as its main gunship and antitank helicopter. It can fly and attack targets day or night, in almost any kind of weather. It is usually armed with 16 laser-guided Hellfire missiles or up to 76 70mm rockets. It also has a 30mm automatic chaingun that shoots up to 1,200 high-explosive bullets.

Apaches are superb tank killers. They are fast, maneuverable, and hard to detect on radar screens. They are sent as a first-wave attack force, clearing the battlefield of enemy tanks so that ground forces can start their attack.

An Apache attack helicopter is refueled at Bagram Air Base, 80 miles (129 km) north of Kabul, Afghanistan.

UH-60 BLACKHAWK HELICOPTER

Primary function: Air assault and general support missions
Speed: 184 mph (296 km/h)
Armament: Two 7.62mm machineguns, 4 Volcano or 16 Hellfire antitank missiles
Crew: Two pilots, one crew chief (one door gunner when required)
Cost: $8 million

The U.S. Army's Blackhawk can lift up to 8,000 pounds (3,629 kg) and fly deep into enemy territory. It can carry up to 14 soldiers and is often used by special forces teams. It is also useful for moving wounded soldiers, search-and-rescue missions, night operations, and scouting enemy positions. Blackhawks include enhanced electronics that help with navigation and self-defense.

Two UH-60 Blackhawk helicopters aboard USS *Kearsarge*

BOMBS AND MISSILES

TOMAHAWK CRUISE MISSILE

Range: 1,000 miles (1,609 km)
Length: 18 to 20 feet (5 to 6 m)
Wingspan: 9 feet (3 m)
Guidance: Uses digital scene matching area correlations, inertial and terrain contour matching, and global positioning system to reach targets
Launch: Launches from ships or submarine torpedo tubes
Cost: $600,000

Tomahawk cruise missiles are guided weapons launched from ships or submarines. They fly like small airplanes, remaining hidden from enemy radar by hugging close to the ground. They can be launched hundreds of miles away, yet hit their targets with great accuracy. Tomahawks can fly at 550 miles per hour (885 km/h), which makes them even more difficult to shoot down. A larger version of cruise missile, the AGM-86B/C is launched from B-52 or B1 bombers.

When a Tomahawk strikes its target, it detonates a 1,000-pound (454 kg) bomb. Because of their accuracy, and because there is no human pilot at risk, cruise missiles are the weapon of choice for the U.S. Department of Defense. It is often used as a first strike weapon, destroying enemy radar and command and control centers. This clears the way for U.S. aircraft and ground forces. Tomahawks were fired at land targets during the 2001–2002 Afghanistan conflict and the 2003 war in Iraq.

The guided-missile destroyer USS *Porter* (DDG 78) launches a Tomahawk
Land Attack Missile (TLAM) toward Iraq on March 22, 2003.

PATRIOT MISSILE

Range: 1,000 miles (1,609 km)
Length: 17 feet (5 m)
Diameter: 16 inches (41 cm)
Wingspan: 20 inches (51 cm)
Launch: Mobile semi-trailer
Cost: $217 million per launcher group

The Patriot is the U.S. Army's mobile surface-to-air defense system. It is used mainly against enemy ballistic missiles, but can also defend against aircraft and cruise missiles. Early versions of the Patriot, such as those used in the 1991 Persian Gulf War, used explosive warheads to destroy incoming targets.

The most recent version of the Patriot, the PAC-3, destroys its target by colliding with it at high speed in mid-air. It uses a sophisticated weapons control computer to track incoming missiles by radar. The PAC-3 Patriot is a vast improvement over earlier models, but it's still not perfect. According to military sources, during the first two weeks of the 2003 war in Iraq, the enemy launched 13 short-range missiles against coalition forces. Eight missiles were intercepted and destroyed by the Patriot missile defense system. Four enemy missiles went off course or blew up shortly after launch. The thirteenth missile got through the Patriot defensive umbrella and hit near a shopping mall in Kuwait City, Kuwait.

A Patriot missile is launched by soldiers of the Eleventh Brigade, Forty-third Air Defense Artillery.

GBU-28 BUNKER BUSTER

Type: 4,700-pound (2,132 kg)
  precision-guided weapon
Length: 19 feet (5.8 m)
Diameter: 14.5 inches (36.8 cm)
Range: Approximately 6 miles
  (10 km)
Penetration: 20 feet (6 m) of
  concrete buildings or
  underground hideouts

The GBU-28 is an accurate bomb designed to burrow into the ground and destroy bunkers or caves where the enemy may be hiding, giving it the nickname Bunker Buster. The GBU-28 is guided to its target by laser beam after being delivered by an F-15 Eagle fighter jet.

The warhead on the GBU-28 explodes after burrowing into the earth. It can penetrate the concrete wall of an underground bunker up to 20 feet (6 m) thick. It can also travel up to 100 feet (30 m) underground. The explosion sucks the air out of any underground tunnel or bunker. Tremendous heat follows, burning or melting anything left inside.

A weapons loader prepares a GBU-31 joint direct attack munition for a mission at a forward-deployed location.

AGM-154 JSOW

Type: Air-to-ground smart bomb

Range: 30 miles (48 km)

Guidance: Can use global positioning system to seek targets

Use: Used to attack targets from outside enemy air defenses

The AGM-154 Joint Standoff Weapon (JSOW) is a 1,000-pound (454 kg) air-to-surface missile. It's guided to its target by highly accurate GPS data. Jets launch JSOWs at a variety of targets, including tanks, buildings, or radar installations. JSOWs are launched at their targets from a distance, which increases the survivability of aircraft.

U.S. Navy sailors inspect AGM air-to-ground smart bombs on the USS *Enterprise*.

JDAM

Global positioning system guidance kit

Converts existing free falling bombs into smart weapons

JDAM stands for Joint Direct Attack Munition. It is a guidance kit that is fitted on regular dumb bombs. The kit includes movable tail fins that guide the bomb using a complex navigation system that uses GPS data. This combination creates a relatively cheap smart bomb that can strike a target, even in bad weather, with surgical precision.

Joint Direct Attack Munitions (JDAM) rest on the flight deck while other munitions are relocated by aviation ordnancemen aboard USS *Kitty Hawk*.

TOOLS OF THE INFANTRY

M16A2 ASSAULT RIFLE

The M16A2 is a 5.56mm assault rifle used by most combat infantry troops. At 8.7 pounds (3.9 kg) it is relatively lightweight, and can be fired from the shoulder or hip. The M16 is designed to be fired once every time the trigger is pulled, or in full automatic mode. It has an effective range up to 2 miles (3 km). It can also be fitted with a night-vision scope and a grenade launcher.

M4A1 CARBINE

The 5.56mm M4 rifle is compact at only 33 inches (84 cm). It's also light, weighing just 7.65 pounds (3.47 kg). It is often used by special forces troops. The M4 rifle features a silencer, night-vision scope, and targeting laser. It can also be equipped with a grenade launcher under the barrel.

MP-5N SUBMACHINE GUN

The MP-5N is a 9mm submachine gun used by Special Forces troops to fight in tight quarters, such as urban assault missions and raids. The MP-5N shoots 800 rounds per minute. It is also a basic weapon for the Federal Bureau of Investigation's Hostage Rescue Team.

BROWNING M2

The Browning M2 is a .50-caliber machine gun. It is a powerful belt-fed, crew-operated weapon. The M2 can be used not only against enemy troops, but also against light armored vehicles and slow-flying aircraft. It can be carried and fired from a tripod. Or, it can be mounted on vehicles or boats.

BERETTA 9MM PISTOL

Lightweight and easy to hide, the Beretta is the general-use pistol of the U.S. military.

REMINGTON MODEL 870 12-GAUGE COMBAT SHOTGUN

This shotgun is used for close-quarter fighting, especially in tight urban environments such as house-to-house combat.

NIGHT-VISION GOGGLES

Night-vision goggles are standard-issue among special operations troops. Many regular combat soldiers also use these goggles. The United States has the best night-vision technology in the world, giving its soldiers a major advantage on the battlefield.

Night-vision goggles collect light and convert it into electrons, similar to how a digital camera works. The electrons are then amplified and projected onto a green phosphor screen. Green is used because the human brain can see details better using that color. This technology allows soldiers to see in even the dimmest starlight. Night-vision technology can also be mounted to a soldier's gun scope.

HELMET

Helmets used by the U.S. military are made of lightweight, high-impact Kevlar plastic. These helmets are so strong, they can stop bullets from assault rifles.

BODY ARMOR

Flak jackets are similar to those worn by Special Weapons and Tactics (SWAT) teams and other police officers. They protect the upper body from bullets and shrapnel. Lightweight Kevlar fragmentation vests protect against injuries from flying shrapnel.

BIO-CHEMICAL SUIT

To protect against some weapons of mass destruction (WMD), American combat troops carry a pouch that contains a gas mask, suit, gloves, and vinyl shoe covers. These suits are called JSLIST, which stands for Joint Service Lightweight Integrated Suit Technology. These suits protect mainly against chemical weapons, but they can be effective against some biological weapons as well.

Each suit weighs about 6 pounds (3 kg) and is said to be effective for up to 45 days. The suits come with a kit that contains atropine, a drug used as an antidote for some nerve-gas attacks. Also included are specially treated moist towelettes for cleaning skin that may have been exposed to chemicals or germs.

The bio-chemical suit must be put on quickly to protect against attack. It is worn over a soldier's regular uniform. The suit is made with layers of fabric containing carbon, which absorbs chemical and biological agents. The suits can be very effective if worn properly, but in the heat of desert warfare, the suits can make soldiers miserable.

Troops in the 2003 war in Iraq were well equipped for the possibility of encountering several kinds of WMD. These included VX nerve gas, which kills by shutting down a person's nervous system; mustard gas, which is a blister agent that causes painful swelling and blisters if inhaled; and Sarin, a nerve agent similar to VX gas. All of these chemical agents could be used by spraying or dispersing in artillery shells, or by contaminating ground areas.

U.S. soldiers wear chemical suits while conducting
a chemical test in the Iraqi desert.

WEB SITES
WWW.ABDOPUB.COM

To learn more about weapons of the twenty-first century, visit ABDO Publishing Company on the World Wide Web at **www.abdopub.com**. Web sites about weapons of the twenty-first century are featured on our Book Links page. These links are routinely monitored and updated to provide the most current information available.

An aviation ordnanceman checks laser-guided bombs before they are loaded onto jets on the USS *Kitty Hawk*.

An aircraft mechanic inspects an A-10 Thunderbolt after a flight.

GLOSSARY

antidote:
A remedy that can counteract the effects of a poison.

carpet bombing:
Dropping many bombs over an area in order to destroy or degrade enemy forces before a ground assault.

casualty:
A person who is either injured or killed in an act of war.

Cold War:
The mainly diplomatic conflict waged between the United States and the former Soviet Union after World War II. The Cold War resulted in a large buildup of weapons and troops. It ended when the Soviet Union broke up in the late 1980s and early 1990s.

dumb bomb:
A bomb, dropped from an airplane, that simply falls to the ground without navigating itself to its target. Since dumb bombs cannot be controlled, they are not always accurate.

fuselage:
The main body of an airplane, minus the wings, tail, and engines.

munitions:
Generally, munitions refer to all war supplies, but mainly refer to bombs and ammunition.

polar orbit:
An orbit that causes satellites to circle the earth from pole to pole, rather than around the equator.

smart bomb:
A bomb or missile that navigates its way to a target, usually by following a laser beam "painted" on the target by a plane or special operations soldier on the ground. Smart bombs are very accurate.

supersonic:
Faster than the speed of sound, which travels at 1,116 feet per second (340 m/s).

warhead:
The forward section of a bomb or missile usually containing an explosive charge. Warheads can also be filled with chemical or biological agents.

weapons of mass destruction (WMD):
Weapons that kill or injure large numbers of people, or cause massive damage to buildings. When people talk about weapons of mass destruction, they are usually referring to nuclear, biological, or chemical weapons.

INDEX